A Glow

"It's puzzling. One never makes a move without the others."

"They're probably still in their litter mentality," Khalia said. "Sometimes it takes a while to come out on your own."

"But it's time. Past time," Shredder said. "I never saw kits that stuck to each other like this. And they don't talk. Not a word."

Khalia had to admit this was odd. Most kits by their age couldn't keep their mouths shut.

"They've got trauma," she decided. "From the highway, when they came across."

"Maybe," Shredder said. "But we've all got that. I've noticed something else."

"What?"

"They have a glow."

"A *what*?"

"A shine. Real faint. You see it best at night."

"What does it mean?"

"I don't know. I never saw anything like it before."

OTHER BOOKS BY JANET TAYLOR LISLE

Afternoon of the Elves

Black Duck

The Lost Flower Children

HIGHWAY
CATS

JANET TAYLOR LISLE

illustrated by

David Frankland

PUFFIN BOOKS
An Imprint of Penguin Group (USA) Inc.

Patricia Lee Gauch, Editor

PUFFIN BOOKS
Published by the Penguin Group
Penguin Group (USA) Inc., 345 Hudson Street, New York, New York 10014, U.S.A.
Penguin Group (Canada), 90 Eglinton Avenue East, Suite 700, Toronto, Ontario, Canada M4P 2Y3
(a division of Pearson Penguin Canada Inc.)
Penguin Books Ltd, 80 Strand, London WC2R 0RL, England
Penguin Ireland, 25 St Stephen's Green, Dublin 2, Ireland (a division of Penguin Books Ltd)
Penguin Group (Australia), 250 Camberwell Road, Camberwell, Victoria 3124, Australia
(a division of Pearson Australia Group Pty Ltd)
Penguin Books India Pvt Ltd, 11 Community Centre, Panchsheel Park, New Delhi - 110 017, India
Penguin Group (NZ), 67 Apollo Drive, Rosedale, North Shore 0632, New Zealand
(a division of Pearson New Zealand Ltd)
Penguin Books (South Africa) (Pty) Ltd, 24 Sturdee Avenue, Rosebank, Johannesburg 2196, South Africa

Registered Offices: Penguin Books Ltd, 80 Strand, London WC2R 0RL, England

First published by Philomel Books, a division of Penguin Young Readers Group, 2008
Published by Puffin Books, a division of Penguin Young Readers Group, 2009

1 3 5 7 9 10 8 6 4 2

Text copyright © Janet Taylor Lisle, 2008
Illustrations copyright © David Frankland, 2008
All rights reserved

THE LIBRARY OF CONGRESS HAS CATALOGED THE PHILOMEL BOOKS EDITION AS FOLLOWS:
Lisle, Janet Taylor.
Highway cats / Janet Taylor Lisle ; illustrated by David Frankland. p. cm.
Summary: A hard-bitten group of mangy highway cats is changed forever
after the mysterious arrival of three kittens.
ISBN: 978-0-399-25070-5 (hc)
1. Cats—Juvenile fiction. [1. Cats—Fiction.] I. Frankland, David, ill. II. Title.
PZ10.3.L68Hi 2008 [Fic]—dc22 2008017165

Puffin Books ISBN 978-0-14-241485-9

Printed in the United States of America
Design by Semadar Megged

For Mary Logan Taylor, who kept this story going.

And for the cats: Hurricane, Boris, Roosevelt, Kayla, Charlotte, Wilbur, and Mrs. Pimpergnaw.
—JTL

To Buster.
—DF

HIGHWAY CATS

SCENE: *Potterberg city hall, evening, high up in the mayor's office. His Honor Mayor Blunt stands at the window gazing down upon the bright city lights of Potterberg while conducting a private conference with his chief of staff, Farley. From outside come traffic noises: honks, sirens, screeching brakes, the hiss and growl of wheels on pavement.*

MAYOR BLUNT. The thing is, Farley, I'm coming up for re-election soon. I need a campaign issue.

FARLEY. Yes, sir, Mayor. You need to have something to point to, some accomplishment so the people of Potterberg will want to vote for you again.

MAYOR. Exactly, Farley. You're my man. Got any ideas?

FARLEY. Well, you know the new shopping center out by the city line? There it is—you can just see it from here. (*Farley points through the window.*)

MAYOR. (*Squinting at a fiery mass of glinting roofs in the distance.*) What about it?

FARLEY. It's growing fast. Another restaurant went in last month. A computer store just opened. They had to double the size of the parking lot.

MAYOR. So?

FARLEY. So it's going to need access.

MAYOR. Access to what?

FARLEY. To the highway. At present, Interstate 95 runs right by, but there's no way to get off. People want an exit ramp so they can get off and go shopping.

MAYOR. Well, naturally!

FARLEY. And an entrance ramp to get back on afterward and go home.

MAYOR. Of course. Just scrubland back there, isn't it?

FARLEY. There's a small woods.

MAYOR. Why can't we cut through it?

FARLEY. Sure! Or level it completely. It's state property, you know, the last of the big Potter farm that was all around here in the old days. Nothing lives there now but a few skunks and some stray cats. We'll get rid of them in a jiffy.

MAYOR. Let's do it. You go after the permits. I'll hire a work crew.

FARLEY. Yes, sir, Mayor. I'll get right on it.

MAYOR. Good man. People will be impressed. I'll be re-elected for sure.

FARLEY. They'll know you're a mover and a shaker!

MAYOR. So they will, Farley. So they will.

(As the scene fades, night traffic noises outside rise to a thunderous, earsplitting roar.)

CHAPTER ONE

First there was fog, then a heavy spring rain. Out on Interstate 95, traffic had been slow and irritable all afternoon. Not until well past 9 P.M. did the flow of vehicles begin to taper off. Crouched in his hiding place beside the eastbound lanes, the old cat Shredder drew his haunches farther under his body and gazed gloomily across the wet pavement.

"Not a bite to eat," he muttered. "Not a morsel of road food all day." Inside his bony ribs, his stomach gave a mournful howl.

Usually by this time of night he'd have tucked

into a couple of half-eaten hot dogs or a mass of ketchupy french fries. Hamburger Heaven, a popular fast-food restaurant, lay about ten miles down the highway, just far enough for travelers to eat their fill and unload the extras out the window. Bad weather meant slim pickings, though. Shredder had lived beside this stretch of highway long enough to know its ways.

He was soaked through, ready to give up and retreat to the woods for cover, when a pickup truck swerved suddenly out of the line of traffic. It bounced onto the scruffy, overgrown center median between the eastbound and westbound lanes and rolled to a stop.

The driver stepped out. He lifted a cardboard box from the pickup's cargo bed, dropped it on the ground and gave it a rough shove with his foot so it skidded away into the bushes. Then he climbed back in the truck and peeled out with shrieking tires. The stink of hot rubber lingered behind in the air.

Shredder raised his short cat nose toward the smell and sniffed, warily at first, then with knowing.

"Hey, Murray, wake up—there's been a delivery."

A large, bristle-haired alley cat stirred in the roadside bushes nearby. "Whad's that?"

"A delivery, I said. Over there on the center strip in the brush."

Murray the Claw raised his ugly head and took in the reek of rubber.

"Don't smell like nuttin' to me. Whadya wake me for?" he growled in his nasal twang. "How many times I godda tell you?—I cross over for burgers and chicken, that's it. Don't give me any of those nasty egg sandwiches."

"I know, but . . ."

"And no pickles. I can't stand pickles."

"Murray! It's a box. Cardboard. I think it might be . . ."

"Shud up, dope. It's old paint cans, probably."

Nevertheless, both cats peered across four lanes of highway to where the mysterious arrival lay, tilted a bit in the bushes. As they watched, the box lurched and pitched all the way over onto its side.

Shredder sat up. He drew his thin, dirty tail closer around himself and narrowed his eyes.

"Something more than paint cans is in there," he told Murray.

A stream of cars barreled past. A tractor-trailer

roared down on them and went by with a blast of wind, flattening their ears. Afterward, there was a break in the traffic. In the hush, a soft, urgent cry could be heard drifting across from the center median.

"I knew it!" Shredder hissed. "Look!"

A small form emerged from under the box and struggled away into weeds. A second form followed, then a third. There was more crying. Or *mewing* rather, for they were kittens, tiny ones, six weeks old at most. They were staggering around in the center strip completely oblivious to the snap of wheels speeding by on either side. Shredder lowered himself to a watchful hunch while Murray stood up on all fours, showing interest at last.

"So, who's your man?" Murray asked. It was a game they liked to play, a kind of terrible red rover, red rover. These weren't the first median drop-offs to come their way. They weren't even the first kittens.

"Don't know yet," Shredder answered.

"You can't wait till the last second to call it like you did with that chinchilla," Murray warned him. "You godda put your bet down now or forget it."

"Okay, I'll bet on the first one."

"The one that made it first outta the box?"

"That's him. He's got more get-up-and-crawl. Wait a minute, he might be going over to westbound." Both cats leaned forward to look. "No, no, he's not," Shredder went on. "There he is, coming back. Who's *your* man?"

Murray purred acidly to himself, calculating the odds of who would and who wouldn't make it across the traffic lanes to safety on their side. He noted the pace of passing vehicles, the chilling breath of the wind, the expressway's slick surface. At last he spoke.

"Nobody is my bet."

"Nobody!" Shredder glanced at him. "You can't say nobody."

"I'm saying it. Look at them. They're pidiful. They can't hardly walk and they godda get across four lanes?"

"That's not fair," Shredder said. "In fact, it's sick. Part of the game is you've got to believe somebody's going to make it. Otherwise, it's no fun."

"I say none," Murray the Claw snarled, raising the one vicious paw for which he was named. His other three were clawless, victims of a hunter's trap many years ago.

"Okay, okay." Shredder backed away. "Anyhow, look. They're getting ready to come!"

Why young things abandoned in the center median could never sit still and wait for help was a mystery to Shredder. They never could, though. He'd seen enough drop-offs to know. Kittens, puppies, hamsters, turtles, possums, skunks, chicks, rabbits, even a baby alligator one time—they all headed blindly for the highway as soon as possible, without any plan for how to get across. It made you wonder what Mother Nature was thinking to allow her babies to act so stupid.

Tonight, lucky for these kits, Interstate 95 was quieter than on a fair-weather evening. Setting out across the first lane, the three kits hit a surprising lull in the traffic before a string of cars zoomed up and passed them on an outside lane. The afterwind from these vehicles confused the kits. They paused and gazed dimly around. Soon they were moving again. On they struggled into the second lane. Shredder was excited to see that his kit was in the lead.

"Ha! Looky there. My bet's going strong," he boasted.

"Ha yourself. He doesn't godda prayer," Murray rasped back. "None of 'em does. Here comes another bunch of cars. And a cement truck! Whoa, Sally, that thing's moving."

The traffic roared by. Shredder and Murray shut their eyes against flying gravel and road grit. When they looked again, the kits were still in the second lane, huddled down near each other but untouched so far.

"Yay! Yahoo!" Shredder cheered his bet on. "Come on, boy, you can do it. Start walking. You've got a lull. Don't sit there huddling—get up!"

"Looks to me like he don't want to leave his liddle sisters behind," Murray the Claw gloated. "Looks to me like he's gonna sit there and take it in the chops, just like them."

"No, he's not! Get up, kitten!"

Another mass of traffic streamed past. Shredder closed his eyes. Afterward, he opened them reluctantly, afraid he was beat. But the kits were still there! They were on the move too, crawling bravely into the third lane.

"Come on, little buddy!" Shredder was up, waving his bet home. "Only one lane to go. Run! You got it! Run for your life!"

In back of him, Murray started snickering because down the road now came two enormous tractor-trailers traveling side by side the way the big ones do sometimes, late at night. The drivers were probably talking on their CBs, kidding around.

Shredder took one look at this advancing wall of steel and knew he was going to lose. The kits had come to a halt in the third lane. They were too frightened to make any headway. Thunderous vibrations from the tractor-trailers were rising up from the road, paralyzing them.

Shredder gulped under his breath. He wondered what Murray would want for his prize this time. The rule was, the winner could ask for one, just one, thing he wanted. The loser had to deliver. The trouble was that Murray always won. Last time, he'd asked for a bullfrog's eye, a fresh one, and Shredder had spent a week tracking the nasty thing down.

With an earsplitting explosion the trucks went by, double wheels heading directly for the spot where the kittens sat cowering. Shredder turned away at the last minute, unable to watch. He heard Murray chuckle.

"That's it for your bet, buster. Squashed fladder than a bladder."

Shredder peeked over his shoulder. The small

huddle was gone, pushed so deep into the pavement that there was no sign of where the kits had been. Shredder stared at the spot. Was it possible so little could be left? He saw no remains at all, not a smudge or a wisp of hide.

A sudden movement a few yards down from him on the roadside caught his eye.

"Murray, look! It's them!"

Murray spun around.

"Well, drad it, I say. Drad and triple drad!"

"They made it! How in the world did they . . . "

"Wait a minute, there's something fishy about this," Murray snarled. "How did they suddenly get all the way over here? They were out there in the third lane frozen to the asphalt five seconds ago."

"Hello, kits! Congratulations! Greetings! Cheerio!" Shredder couldn't believe he'd won. He was leaping about, wild with joy. The kits, looking dazed and uncertain, were just beginning to get up and sniff the sandy edge of the road, where they had landed in a heap near some yellow grass tufts. Murray was fuming. He looked ready to finish them off himself.

"It's not right! Something's not right!" he protested. "There's been outside inderference here—I can smell it."

"You're just sore you got beat."

"Whadya want for your prize, moron? A brain transplant?" Murray snapped. He was a terrible loser, probably from winning all the time.

"I don't know! I can't think right now. Can I tell you later?"

"Any time, meadball. For the record, though, I'm saying it was fixed."

"Fixed?"

"Those kiddens were headed for oblivion. Somebody went out there and saved them. I don't know who, and I didn't see nuttin', but I know when something's fishy." Murray slouched off into the woods.

Shredder was too glad he'd won to care if anything was fishy or not. He went over to the kits and sniffed happily around them.

"You guys had good luck," he informed them. They were too little to understand, but he told them anyhow.

"You got a break that most don't get, so make the most of it, okay? Take care of yourselves. Don't be hanging around here by the road. Go get some grub. The dump's over there. There!"

The kits weren't catching on to this, so Shredder leaned down and pushed them with his paw until their noses were pointed in the right direction. It didn't help. They turned back the moment he stepped away, sending out a pathetic chorus of mews.

"Don't follow me! Go that way," Shredder urged them, pointing one more time. The hour had come for him to move up the expressway to look for early-morning doughnuts near the overpass. "And stay away from that road!" he called as he padded out of sight.

It might seem heartless to some, leaving senseless babies on a roadside like that, but things worked differently out here by the highway. Shredder knew that he had already done more than most cats would in this outcast place. Everyone for himself—that was the only law here. The faster you learned it, the more chance you had to survive.

CHAPTER TWO

The dump Shredder had pointed the kits toward wasn't the old-fashioned kind of fiery heap reeking of smoke on the edge of town. It was a more-modern place, a group of three enormous, wide-open Dumpsters parked off to one side of the very same thriving shopping center Mayor Blunt had looked down on from his lofty office.

Occupying quarters in this shopping center were, among other stores, Charlotte's Web House (a home computer store), The Three-Minute Egg Roll (a Chinese fast food place), O Solo Mealo (an Italian pizza parlor), and Grill Me, Honey! (a cowboy-style rib house), all in profitable operation serving customers until late into the night. As

a result, there was always an interesting selection of half-chewed egg rolls, rancid meatballs and mildewed ribs lying around in the Dumpsters. On the strength of this, and with the added support of the interstate's road food, a few dozen cats had taken up residence in an overlooked stretch of woods that lay between the shopping center and the highway.

They were a scrawny, scruffy bunch, the kind of cats that couldn't get along in civilized society and now, with the new Dumpsters, didn't have to anymore. Some were runaways who'd been kicked around once too often by their owners. Others had been transported to strange towns and abandoned or left behind when their families moved to the city. That was fine with them. They didn't need families anymore. They'd grown used to living outside on their own. The idea of coming home every night to an overheated kitchen and a bowl of store-bought cat pellets wasn't high on their list of priorities.

Shredder looked tough, but he was an old cat now with an old cat's sadder and deeper thoughts. Compared to Murray the Claw and the rest of the highway bunch, he wasn't much of a ruffian anymore. The foul language that came out of the mouths of these cats was shocking and unprintable. The battles they fought against each other were savage. The rotten stuff they ate and the way they ate it was revolting beyond words, and since they'd long ago stopped washing up like proper cats, they were malodorous, which means they stank. For the most part, they were avoided by humans and animals alike, left to occupy their patch of forest in lowlife peace.

Until they broke the peace, that is. Then there was Animal Control. From time to time AnCon officers were called in to sweep across the parking lot and stop fights. They arrested stragglers, bagged escapees, broke up the biggest brawls with fire hoses and attempted to stamp down the bushes and undergrowth where many cats made their homes. Those who were caught were sent straight to The Shelter, never to return as far as anyone knew.

"What happens there?" a young stray dared to ask one time.

"Curtains is what happens," Murray the Claw had growled. "The lights go out."

"You mean . . . ?"

"Thad's right. And no applause neither."

This was the frightening, grown-up world the kits were about to enter, if they ever smartened up enough to figure out where the Dumpsters were. Now they seemed too exhausted to be hungry. After old Shredder had gone, they curled up together in a soft mound on the side of the highway and went to sleep. When they woke up, it was morning and Khalia Koo was there watching them, along with her sidekick, Jolly Roger. This did not bode well for the kits at all.

Khalia Koo was a once-beautiful Siamese cat who'd been thrown into a fire by a mean-tempered owner and set ablaze. Afterward, though she survived, her face was ruined and she'd turned bitter toward the world. She'd gone into hiding in the little woods and taken to wearing various plastic containers over her head to conceal the horror of her scars. At the moment when the kits woke up, she was wearing a twelve-ounce strawberry yogurt container with the eyeholes gnawed out.

"Well, well, what is this-ss we have here?" she asked Jolly Roger, her blue eyes glittering through the gnaw holes. Inside the container, her *s*'s echoed with an unnerving hiss.

Jolly Roger was used to that. He was a brutish yellow cat with a mouthful of rotten teeth, known for paralyzing his enemies just by smiling.

"Kittens, my dear," he answered, grinning horribly, "but so small you'd hardly know it. Good for nothing, I'd say."

"Not so fas-sst." Khalia Koo paused over the kits. To make a living, she ran a rat farm back in the woods, and finding good help was hard. The highway cats were undependable workers. They'd gobble up a rat on the sly before it was anywhere near fat enough for market, which cut into the profits. Khalia Koo sold rat meat to a pet food company in the city. It was a new item, Canned Rodent, on the supermarket shelves and still making a name for itself. Khalia Koo had high hopes for her business, though.

"We might put the kits to work as trainees-ss," she hissed. "Mold their minds the right way and they'll be ours for life. We wouldn't have to pay them either. They're undercrage."

Jolly Roger smiled. "They'd probably just die on you. They're runty little things—look at their legs."

"Well, how about selling them as overgrown rats-ss? Looks like they've got meat on them." Khalia Koo stuck out a claw and jabbed one of the girl kits in the haunch.

"Ow!" shrieked the kit.

"Hmmm. Not as much there as I thought," Khalia Koo said. "Fuzz mostly. We could use them for pillow stuffing."

"Dead or alive?" Jolly Roger asked.

"Well, dead they wouldn't need feeding. But alive they'd give out heat. It's been a cold spring. How'd you like a pre-warmed pillow to get into bed with at night?"

Jolly Roger smiled and smiled at this. In short order, the kits were captured and dragged back to Khalia Koo's rat farm, a horrid place where the meat rats were kept in wire cages built several feet above the ground, out of reach of passing carnivores, including their own guards.

The kits were thrown into a tiny pen at the back. They cowered together, nibbling bits of skunk cabbage and stale bread that were tossed in after them. Anyone could see they weren't going to last long under these conditions. To make matters worse, that night Khalia Koo and Jolly Roger stuffed them into pillowcases and went to sleep on them.

Shredder heard about it. The next day, he went by the kits' pen and shook his head.

"It's a shame, a shame. After these kits were miraculously saved on the highway and all, now you're going to finish them off like common field rats?" He gazed accusingly at Khalia Koo.

"Mind your own business-ss!" she hissed through the lime sherbet container she was wearing that day. "They get the same treatment as every other cat around here."

"Well, they're too young to stand it," Shredder said. "They'll shrivel up and die. Then you'll have a miracle on your conscience. You'll have gone and snuffed out a miracle."

"A miracle? Rat-wash!" Khalia Koo laughed. She'd heard the story of the kits' amazing crossing but didn't give it much credit. "These kits had blind luck, that's all. They're no more ss-special than anyone els-sse."

Shredder twitched his grizzled tail. "Maybe they are and maybe they aren't. All I'm saying is, what happened out there wasn't usual. They were goners, and then in one blink they were safe. Ask Murray the Claw—he saw the whole thing."

Perhaps she did consult Murray because, later, the sharp eyes of a cottage cheese container could be seen examining the kits from behind a tree. That night, Khalia Koo was careful not to roll too hard on them in her pillow. Next morning, she gave them a sweet-and-sour shrimp that Jolly Roger had unearthed in one of the Dumpsters. It was old and smelly, but the kits gobbled it up.

When Shredder went by again at the end of the

week, the kittens had put on weight. They didn't look too bad, he noticed; a little sad, maybe, from being tossed out so suddenly on their own. They weren't complainers, though, like some. Shredder admired that. He wasn't a complainer either.

"Where are you guys from?" he asked, leaning over their pen in a friendly way that wasn't his usual style. It had been a long time since he'd been near any kittens.

They couldn't answer, of course. They were still too young. They recognized him from the highway, though, and gazed at him with such eager, trusting eyes that he glanced away in embarrassment.

"Don't look at me like that. There's nothing more I can do," he growled, and went off into the woods determined to put them out of his mind.

That evening, though, crouched at the highway's windy edge, Shredder found his thoughts circling back to the kittens with a strange feeling of . . . was it *warmth*? That would never do! He flicked his tail fiercely and turned back to the wind and the roar of traffic.

KHALIA KOO'S RAT FARM was the only cat-owned business for miles around. Most highway cats found it necessary to work for her from time to time, when pickings at the Dumpsters froze up or the highway was rained out. The kits hadn't been at the farm very long before their arrival was noticed and began to stir up talk. After all, every cat in those woods had personal dealings with Interstate 95. Like a powerful river, it flowed down the center of their lives, sometimes giving, sometimes taking away, delivering food and comfort one day, sudden death the next. Among the highway cats, close calls were proof of courage and something to boast about.

"I survived an oil truck going seventy-five miles an hour."

"Well, I outran a horse van and only lost three whiskers."

"A forty-foot camper went right over me in the center lane! I jumped up on its tailpipe and took a ride!"

"That's impossible! Campers don't have tailpipes."

"Well, this one did!"

"Liar!"

"Bonehead!"

"Fur ball!"

"Toad!"

Here the conversation would usually disintegrate into an exchange of claws and teeth.

The kits' crossing sent a ripple of excitement through the cat community. Never had an entire litter of kittens, tiny infants, no less, been so fortunate as to come across together, without injury, when all hope was dashed and rescue seemed impossible. Who were the little survivors? Everyone wanted to know. How did they get so lucky?

Shredder had an answer to that. "It wasn't luck. It was a miracle!" he declared to anyone who would listen. "If you'd been there, you'd have seen. These kittens are something special. There's no other way to explain it."

Of course, there *was* another way. Murray the Claw, still angry about losing his bet, was against all miracles. Holding to his theory of things being fixed and fishy, he talked against the kits whenever possible, making them out to be weaklings of low intelligence, hardly worth the fur they came wrapped in. That didn't stop the buzz, though. As word of the little ones spread, even cats who had never worked at the rat farm, those too ornery or too independent to sign on to a day job, came by to look at them in their pen. When Khalia came out to feed the kits at night, she'd had to wade through a crowd.

"Go on. Get out of here!" she'd snap. "What's a bunch of hard-nosed, flea-bitten characters like you want with kittens? Stand back. Give them some air!"

Grumbling and snarling, the cats would back off. A minute later, they'd close in again. Miracles were things they hadn't seen much of in their lives.

The kits seemed completely unaware of the stir they were causing. They went determinedly about the business of being kittens. They ran. They pounced. They rolled and bit. They were far too young, apparently, to know who or what had rescued them, or to wonder why they were here in this godforsaken place and what would happen next. They were so tiny and so obviously incapable of escape that after a while, Khalia Koo didn't bother to keep them penned up anymore. She allowed them to wander the farm freely during the day.

They went just about everywhere. With their big, curious eyes they examined the cages where the rats were housed together. They visited the feeding machines and the weighing scales and surveyed, with the most innocent expressions, a pile of leftover tails.

"Scram!" "Bug off!" "Whatcha staring at, Twinkie face?" the cat workers snarled, embarrassed to be seen in such a nasty line of work. From the corners of their eyes, they examined them, though. The kits' fur was patchy and their claws had no length. They couldn't hiss or growl, leap or attack. They had none of the skills necessary for a serious highway cat to survive in the world, and yet here they were, cheerfully carrying on. What was it about this that fascinated the cats?

Whatever it was, the workers soon found themselves cleaning up their language around the kits. They cut back on spitting and fighting. A few cats even went so far as to tidy their coats and brush up their whiskers, as if they were hoping to impress the little nitwits.

The other cats sneered loudly when these dandies first showed up among them. No highway cat had ever bothered with appearances before. Dirt was a badge of honor, ticks and fleas the price of freedom. Not long after, however, a wave of grooming swept the farm. Ruffians who had never been associated with "style" suddenly reported for work with sleek legs and bouffant tails. Soon the whole rat farm was looking cleaner, acting better and running more efficiently. Rat-gobbling on the sly (always a messy affair) largely disappeared. Production was picking up!

Being a sharp businesswoman, Kahlia Koo noticed. One day, when no one was looking, she moved the kits out of their tiny pen into the main house with her.

"Who'd ever guess-ss you little ninnies would be s-ssuch a hit?" she hissed at them through the margarine tub she was wearing that day. That night, she excused them from pillow duty.

"Going soft in your old age?" Jolly Roger teased her, baring a yellow fang through his whiskers.

"Clam up," said Khalia. "They're a good invess-ss-tment, that's all, fit for better than to lie under your muddy jowls."

"Who says I have muddy jowls?" Jolly Roger took a swipe at the nearest kit.

"I say!" Khalia replied, giving him a whack on the head.

That night when Shredder stopped by, he noticed that the kits had been served fresh grilled tuna for dinner, while Jolly Roger, smiling murderously, was gnawing on the ancient, meatless spine of a boiled catfish.

CHAPTER THREE

Shredder began to stop in more often at the rat farm.

"You again, Grandpop?" Jolly Roger snickered. "You got a sweetheart somewhere here?"

"Bottle it, maggot face."

"A little touchy, aren't we?"

"We are not!"

As far as anyone knew, Shredder wasn't the sort of cat who cared to attach himself to anyone or any-

thing. He'd certainly never had a sweetheart. The way he told it, he'd been a traveler for most of his life. Abandoned as a newborn on the streets of New Orleans, he'd taken to the road earlier than most, heard the call of the wild and never looked back.

"I'm a one-cat band and plan to stay that way," he liked to boast.

"How'd you get all the way up here?" Khalia Koo asked him once.

"Came up the Mississippi on boats and barges," he answered. "Took me a couple of years just to make it to St. Louis. I stowed away on a steamer in Cairo, Illinois, and went up the Ohio. A cold-blooded river cat I was, outside the law and ruthless as they come. Nobody could lay a hand on me."

He glanced at Khalia to be sure she was appreciating this violent description of his character.

"And then?"

Shredder looked away. "Let's say I caught a bus and came here."

"Caught a bus? How'd you do that?"

"It caught me, actually," Shredder had to admit. "I got locked in the baggage compartment. Big mistake. Four days in the heat of summer without water. I nearly bought it that time."

"No wonder you're so tough."

"You better believe it!"

Khalia Koo smiled under the orange juice container that was her disguise that day. She knew a thing or two about hiding old wounds and had guessed that Shredder might be keeping a secret.

"What's this I hear about you being someone's respectable family pet once, with a roof over your head and a blanket in the corner?"

Shredder squinted sharply. "It's a lie," he snarled.

"I thought so." Khalia shrugged. "I didn't think anybody as tough as you could stand living with that nonsense."

"That's right—they couldn't."

Inside her container, Khalia Koo smiled her knowing smile again.

TRY AS HE MIGHT TO KEEP to the highway rules of turning a cold eye, Shredder found he couldn't stay away from the kittens.

He began inventing reasons for going by the farm. He was picking something up, he'd say, or leaving something off. Once he got there, he'd look around for the kits. There was nothing in it, he told himself. They were his winning bet, that's all. He was interested to see if they could keep on beating the odds.

The kits watched out for Shredder too. When they saw him coming, their eyes lit up and they'd run over each other trying to get to him. It gave the old cat a good feeling to see that. He'd glance around to be sure no one was watching and tickle them under their chins. A minute later, he'd be playing tag or rolling on the grass, as full of high spirits as a youngster himself. He'd take them into the woods, show them a skunk or how to tell north and south from the slant of the sun. Kits should know things like that, shouldn't they? Who else was going to teach them?

Small and scraggly as the little forest was, it was a pretty place to scamper around in. The trees were old and tall, sheltering the nests of many songbirds and climbing animals. Spicy-smelling pine needles lay thick on the ground, warmed by sunshine that shafted through a latticework of branches above.

That spring, tiny flowers appeared along what might once have been woodland paths if anyone had been there to walk them. No one was anymore.

The shopping center was where people walked now, while what remained of the forest's wild creatures followed ancient routes of their own.

The highway cats, more recently arrived, walked apart and alone. Their paths were random, winding through brambles and thickets, around stumps and fallen trees, past bogs and anthills, across a pebbly brook that rattled from a freshwater spring at the heart of the wood. Nearby, on a small hill long lost to outside eyes, a mossy stone wall enclosed an abandoned graveyard. Potter, its crumbling headstones read, hieroglyphics to the cats. They scampered past without a glance.

A grove of tall pines grew off to one side. Shredder began to take the kittens there for climbing lessons.

"Climb in a circle—don't go straight up," he advised them. "With a regular tree, you can jump branch to branch. With a pine, it's dense. You've got to work your way up."

The kits tried to follow directions.

"Not bad. Practice in your spare time," he encouraged them. Privately, he worried: they seemed strangely slow. They couldn't keep control of their feet and tended to lose their balance in a most uncat-like way. There was a second problem too. They always wanted to stick together.

Shredder mentioned it to Khalia Koo one day.

"It's puzzling. One never makes a move without the others."

"They're probably still in their litter mentality," Khalia said. "Sometimes it takes a while to come out on your own."

"But it's time. Past time," Shredder said. "I never saw kits that stuck to each other like this. And they don't talk. Not a word."

Khalia had to admit this was odd. Most kits by their age couldn't keep their mouths shut.

"They've got trauma," she decided. "From the highway, when they came across."

"Maybe," Shredder said. "But we've all got that. I've noticed something else."

"What?"

"They have a glow."

"A *what*?"

"A shine. Real faint. You see it best at night."

"What does it mean?"

"I don't know. I never saw anything like it before."

That night, Khalia Koo spied on the kits in the dark of her kitchen as they slept in their usual mound. She saw that Shredder was right. A faint silvery blue sparkle surrounded them, drifting up off their coats like early-morning mist over a pond.

Beneath the designer tissue box she was wearing that evening, her Siamese eyes narrowed in alarm. She was on the verge of calling for Jolly Roger to throw the whole bunch from her house—a job he would have relished!—when one of the girl kits woke up. As Khalia watched, she opened her tiny mouth in a wide, pink yawn, gave a sigh of contentment and fell back asleep against her brother and sister.

Khalia's call died on her lips. She tiptoed out of the room and crept away to bed with a softness in her heart she hadn't felt in years.

It didn't last. How could it? Such memories were useless in a place like this. The sun was barely up before the businesslike shape of a manila envelope (with two eyeholes gnawed out) could be seen through her windows, bent over piles of account books and sales sheets.

"It's a good thing those kits improve my rat production. Anyone else with sparkle would be out my door in twenty-five seconds," she snapped at Shredder when he came by. "I can't afford to fool around with mystical stuff."

"Sure," Shredder agreed. "You've got orders to fill."

"And a company to run."

"You have to look out for yourself."

"Exactly. I can't be wasting time chasing after a bunch of kittens! I've half a mind to throw them out the door tonight."

"Tonight," Shredder cried. "But they've nowhere else to go!"

"Maybe it's-ss time they did!" Khalia said, with such an alarming hiss that Shredder knew he must take immediate action. For better or worse, the moment had come to introduce his tiny friends to the dump.

"You guys need to learn how to feed yourselves," he explained to them that afternoon as they poked around the old cemetery.

The kits were acting especially kittenish that day, hiding under vines and leaping out to chase butterflies between the graves. They'd discovered the remains of a house foundation jutting out of the ground and not far away a pile of giant timbers that might once have belonged to a barn. They practiced jumps from the timbers, making no improvement that Shredder could see.

"Stop that and listen!" he ordered. "You've had an amazing run up to now: crossing the highway, getting moved indoors, eating high off the hog. It can't go on. Nothing like that ever lasts."

The kits rubbed playfully against him, as if to protest this harsh view of the world, but for once Shredder pushed them away.

"You've got to grow up! I won't always be here to look after you."

That night, he took the kits out of Khalia's house (while she pretended to look the other way) and marched them sternly through the woods to the shopping center to begin their instruction.

THEY ARRIVED ABOUT MIDNIGHT, just as the restaurants were closing. Several loads of unusually fine garbage had been dumped during the day, and a fair number of highway cats were there rooting around inside the Dumpsters, seizing greasy morsels and dragging them up onto the high metal sides to devour them. Competition was fierce. Bad-tempered snarls and hisses came from all corners.

The kits hung back from this threatening scene. Shredder prodded them forward.

"Come on! You've got to show some grit if you want to eat around here."

He demonstrated how to climb up to the Dumpster's metal rim and spy out for juicy tidbits inside. The kits followed him shakily. They were just beginning to get their balance and look around when an ugly head reared up from a carcass below.

"So, id's Shredder with his nursery school phonies," Murray the Claw called out in his tough-guy twang. "Welcome, toddlers!" He lifted his one vicious paw in a sarcastic salute.

"Ciao, Murray. What's going down?" Shredder replied coldly. He'd picked up some foreign words during his travels across the country. Murray was not impressed.

"Chow *is* what's going down, dimwid. Beijing duck, to be precise. You dwerps planning any miracles tonight?" he sneered at the kits, who retreated unsteadily behind Shredder.

The cats around them snickered.

"Leave them alone," Shredder warned. "They don't know anything."

"Maybe," purred Murray. "Or maybe not. I've been hearing about these freeloaders, how they're in the house with Khalia Koo, eating her food. Now thad really is a miracle."

The highway cats snickered again. Several moved up closer. They smelled a fight brewing.

"Lay off," Shredder warned, but Murray went right on.

"So, let's get to the boddom of this," he said. He leapt up on the Dumpster's high edge and began walking around it, Egyptian style, to confront Shredder. "We're all a liddle confused. We want to see what these miracle phonies are made of. Can they dance, for instance?"

Murray's sharp claw paw zipped out and smacked the kits behind Shredder so hard they hopped up in the air just as if they were dancing.

The highway cats howled with laughter.

"Hey!" yelled Shredder. "Quit that!" But Murray wouldn't.

"Can they sing?" he asked, reaching out and pricking their little ears.

"Eee, eee, eee," wailed the kits in unison.

The highway cats laughed louder.

"Stop it!" shouted Shredder. He tried to punch Murray, but the old bristle hair scooted out of reach.

"And most of all, what I want to know is: CAN THEY FLY?" roared Murray, darting toward them again. He caught the kits with the tips of his claws and launched them, one after another, off the Dumpster's metal edge and high into the air, where they surprised everyone by plummeting like stones, headfirst, toward the ground. Not only was there no miracle flight, they showed none of the airborne grace of even the most ordinary alley cat.

At this, Shredder lunged at Murray and began to fight him. The other highway cats, who'd been spoiling for a brawl anyway, leapt on Shredder ("Fakes, fakes!" they howled) and then on each other. Soon the shopping center Dumpsters were boiling inside and out with furious clawing, biting cats and wild screeches, and bloodcurdling yowls went out in all directions.

Across the parking lot, several automobiles came to a halt. A crowd of late-night diners gathered outside the restaurants. Never had they seen such a savage horde of cats.

Soon sirens wailed and Animal Control pulled up in an armored, grill-windowed vehicle, followed by a fire engine and a police car. Within minutes, AnCon officers had rushed across the parking lot and were wading into the fray. They walloped the fighting cats with sticks and kicked them with their heavy boots while the firemen aimed fire hoses and blasted the Dumpsters with water.

The highway cats were in such a maddened state by this time that at first nothing would stop them. Not until AnCon officers had succeeded in slipping bags over the heads of a few brawlers did the danger begin to sink in.

"Run for it! AnCon!" The cry went up at last. The cats were jolted back to their senses. Doused and bedraggled, they fled in a tangled, clawing mass toward the shelter of the woods. Shredder went with them, limping from a bite wound on his front leg. His pain was so great that he forgot about the kits. Only at the forest's edge did he suddenly remember and turn back.

It was too late. In the midst of the chaos he saw the little ones huddled desperately together, not far from where they had landed after their plunge from the Dumpster. As he watched, two AnCon officers bore down on them, bags in hand.

"Look out!" Shredder shrieked. "Run! Run for your lives!"

The kits didn't hear. They cringed in terror, unable to move. It was just as it had been on the highway when Shredder and Murray had played their gruesome game. Now as then, Shredder closed his eyes and held his breath, though this time there was no bet to be won from their escape. When he looked again, the terrible deed was done. The kits were gone. The officers, clutching their wriggling bags, were marching off to look for other stragglers.

A cold fist took hold of Shredder's heart and squeezed.

WHILE THE OTHER CATS FLED, Shredder stayed behind that night, crouched in tall grass on the edge of the parking lot. He couldn't make himself run away.

He saw the AnCon officers give up their chase, get into their grill-windowed vehicle and drive off. He watched the firemen and the police car depart and the crowd of spectators break up and head for home. Only when the last human had gone and the parking lot lay gleaming under its all-night lights did he step out, a tiny, limping shadow on the vast field of cement. He went across to the spot where the kits had been, sniffing here and there.

"Where are you guys?" he whispered. "Now's the time to show your stuff. If you're here, come out. You can come out now."

A lone dog bayed in a nearby yard. A chilly wind blew across the parking lot, rattling the branches of the little forest. Through the trees, Shredder heard a truck horn's mournful hoot out on the highway. From the kits, there was no answer.

The old cat put his head down and limped away. As he went, a black despair spread through him, and the whole of his life seemed to rise before his eyes. He saw the careless streets of New Orleans and the treacherous river barges. He saw the door of a bus baggage compartment close on him with a slam. He felt the angry, beating sticks of AnCon's officers and the fire hose's blast, and it seemed to him that the world had no place for him, that he was doomed always to live hungry and alone, cast out along the highway like a useless piece of trash.

Shredder began to run. Faster he went, faster and faster, until the hot glare of the parking lot was left behind and he was deep in the dark bushy arms of the forest.

•••••••••••••••

SCENE: *Early the next morning (5 A.M.) at Mayor Blunt's Potterberg home. His Honor is jolted awake in bed by a ringing telephone. He answers to find Chief of Staff Farley on the line.*

MAYOR BLUNT. Uff?

FARLEY. Mayor? Mayor, is that you?

MAYOR. Ump!

FARLEY. Sorry to wake you, sir. There's been an incident. I thought you might want to know so you'll be ready for the television reporters this morn—

MAYOR. (*Still half asleep.*) Oog grumph!

FARLEY. Yes, sir, I know it's early. There's been an incident with a few cats. Well, a lot of cats, actually. Out in that shopping center by the highway. They came from the woods there. A big fight at the Dumpsters.

MAYOR. Awk!

FARLEY. Yes, people were frightened. We've had complaints. It's all right now. Animal Control did its job. But we need to keep a handle on the press. They'll be raising issues of rampant rabies, roving wildcats, town leadership asleep at the helm.

MAYOR. Glickenclopencope!

FARLEY. What's that, Mayor? I didn't quite catch . . .

MAYOR. GLICKENCLOPENCOPE!

FARLEY. Of course, sir. Understood. Your leadership *never* sleeps. You're on top of everything 24/7, 7/52, and 12/1. What I was thinking was, this might be a good time to announce your new exit ramp plan. That woods demolition crew can be ready to go at the end of this week. You could kill two birds with one . . .

MAYOR. (*Yawning*) Ugoocatskulldone.

FARLEY. *What?* Oh . . . haw, haw, that's a good one. Two *cats* with one stone. Right. Don't worry, we'll get rid of the little pests. They won't know what hit 'em. I'll give the order to proceed, let you get back to your rest. You want to be ready for the TV reporters in the morning. Not to mention the camera crew and the *Potterberg Evening News* and a conference call with the National Guard . . .

(*Farley jabbers on. The mayor's eyelids flutter and close. He begins to snore, a low rumble that grows into a thunderous roar, as the scene fades.*)

CHAPTER FOUR

As dawn broke in the little forest, a long roll of thunder echoed ominously through the air. The wild creatures who lived there glanced up in alarm. A storm was coming. A bad one! Though it seemed still some way off, the animals started to prepare.

They sent warning calls to their neighbors, gathered their young, stockpiled food and began to burrow into thickets or the hollows of rotted logs. Above, in the trees, the birds also were on guard, crying to each other in shrill voices and making for shelter in the dense groves of pine.

Only out on the highway were there no calls of

alarm. The cats lying in wait for breakfast cared nothing for each other or the weather. The roar of wheels was in their ears. The wind from passing cars flattened the fur against their heads. Who could watch the sky when a bulging bag of sausage biscuits might land at any moment in the center lane? Everyone for himself, that was the rule out here, and those who forgot it would lose out to those who knew better.

About mid-morning, as dark clouds moved closer, the lean, rectangular form of a cereal box slid out of the woods. It made its way toward the highway's edge, halting at a place where a particularly ratty-looking tail could be seen sticking out of a clump of weeds.

"Murray the Claw! Is that you?"

"Yeah, it's me. Whadya want, a Coco Pop in the nose? Ha, ha, ha."

Khalia Koo gazed at him with extreme dislike. Whatever sympathy she might have felt for Murray's mutilated paws was always quickly erased by his sneering attitude.

"I'm looking for my kittens-ss," she told him. "They didn't come home last night. Any sign of them here?"

Murray turned his furry bulk around to face her. He gave another guffaw.

"AnCon caught 'em," he said. "At the Dumpsters. We all saw it. Those liddle miracles got the sack. I say good riddance to bad rubbish."

"They didn't run," added Jolly Roger, appearing from a nearby bush with a savage smile. He and Murray had formed an alliance of sorts. It was based on their mutual dislike of all kittens everywhere, especially highway drop-offs who pretended to be special.

"Your kits sat blinking like morons in the path of certain destruction," Jolly Roger went on. "What could anyone do?"

"You could've tried to ss-save them," Khalia Koo hissed, sounding more upset than one might expect of a cold-blooded business-cat. "Where's Shredder?"

"Holed up somewhere. Not speaking to no one." Murray snickered again. "He lost his bet in the end, that's for sure. Nobody's likely to set eyes on those liddle twids again."

Khalia felt a sudden, powerful urge to sink her teeth into Murray's back. She was a civilized cat, though, who believed in higher standards of behavior. Besides, she realized that Murray was right. Sad as it was, the kits were most likely history. Their small miraculous lives had come and gone like rays of sun on a rainy day. Under the cereal box, she allowed herself a small, damp sniff. Then she pulled herself together.

"Why are you hanging around with this-ss one-clawed weas-ssel," she hissed at Jolly Roger. "He'll just get you into trouble. Come on back to the farm with me. We've got work to do."

"Not me. I quit," the yellow cat snapped. "I'm eating better out here on the road and getting more respect. You and your rat business can go to the moon for all I care!" He turned his back on her and refused to budge.

Khalia Koo went home alone with a dark and friendless feeling. Even after the storm dwindled into light rain and the sun came out in a golden glow, she huddled inside her kitchen. It wasn't only that Jolly Roger had turned against her. Without the kits running around, getting underfoot, the whole house seemed suddenly so cold and empty.

KHALIA WASN'T THE ONLY one to notice the kittens' absence. At the rat farm that afternoon, the cat workers were moody. They'd heard about the kits' capture and kept glancing toward their old pen, as if they expected the little ones to show up anyway.

All that day, they watched for them, and the next day and the next. When, after a week, it became clear that no further miracles were at hand and the kits were truly lost, the workers became sullen and bad-tempered. Their foul vocabularies returned. They scratched and fought among themselves. No one bothered to wash up anymore and rat-gobbling rose to heights of gluttony never seen before at the farm.

As if this weren't enough, even the rats went into a gray funk. They lay on the wiry bottoms of their cages, clamped their mouths shut and refused to eat. Within days they became so thin that pet food production was brought to a halt. There was no work to be done anymore. Khalia Koo was forced to let her cat crew go. One by one, the cats slunk away toward the highway or to the Dumpsters, followed shortly by droves of rats, which, in their new scrawniness, were able to slip through the wires of their cages and escape.

So the once-thriving rat farm was deserted.

Shredder, arriving at the farm one morning several days later, found Khalia Koo perched on the roof of one of her own rat cages, surveying her ruined business through the dusty mesh of an empty potato sack.

"Where've you been?" she called to him. "Hiding out, I hear. A lot of help you are in the face of disaster!"

She turned her back angrily on him.

The old cat climbed up beside her. His coat was ragged and thick with mud. His whiskers were frayed. He looked exhausted.

"I wasn't hiding. I was traveling. I've been to The Shelter."

"The SSS-Shelter!" Khalia glanced around. No one she knew and no one she'd ever heard of had made the trip downtown to The Shelter. The stranglehold of highways around Potterberg guaranteed death to all who tried to enter on foot.

"Why did you go there?"

"To look for the kits."

"To rescue them, I suppose. What a hare-brained idea."

Shredder nodded and hung his head. "I was hoping I might at least talk to them, through the walls or something. I couldn't stand the thought of them locked up alone." Shredder's voice began to tremble. "Shut away in that place for weeks and weeks with no one to help . . . no one, no one . . . " He broke down and couldn't go on.

Khalia's heart went out to him. She knew he was remembering his own loneliness and the terrifying journey in the baggage compartment.

"Did you find them?" she asked gently.

Shredder shook his head. "They weren't there. I went over every one of the AnCon vehicles, double-checked every door into the place. The kits never made it inside. If they had, I'd have smelled them."

"So, where are they?"

"Gone. Lost. AnCon must've gotten rid of them on the way."

"Gotten rid of them! How?"

"Better not to think of that."

There was a long silence during which both cats thought of it anyway.

"Well, ss-so much for your miracles-ss," Khalia hissed bitterly at last.

"The kits' luck finally ran out," Shredder had to agree.

"I always-ss knew it would. Jus-ss-st a matter of time."

"Such tiny things. I don't know why I put my hopes on them."

"They ss-seemed to be doing okay for a while. I was kind of hopeful myself," Khalia admitted.

"We tried to look after them."

"We did."

"They were too young, that's all. Too innocent. They didn't stand a chance in this rotten place."

"None of us does, when you think about it," Khalia couldn't help blurting out. "Here we are, cornered, in this tiny patch of woods, surrounded on all sides by asphalt and cement. It won't last, you can bet. It never does for cats like us. The world will catch up and chase us out again."

She had hardly finished speaking when, as if to underline the truth of her words, a frightening roar rose from the direction of the shopping center parking lot. Both cats leapt to their feet. A huge bulldozer hove into view, smashing through the trees and squashing bushes left and right. Behind it, a team of long-stemmed, beetle-browed humans advanced on foot, making directly for them. The two cats had only moments to evacuate to a nearby oak before the machine had flattened the rat cages and proceeded to carve a red-brown swath of newly turned earth across Khalia Koo's farm.

The noise was hideous. Sound waves echoed through the forest, sending flocks of birds spiraling upward into the sky and small animals scooting underground.

Khalia and Shredder clung to their tree in terror while the bulldozer plowed through a stone wall and, continuing on, headed for an innocent clump of blue flowers nestled in a clearing beyond. Shredder shut his eyes. It was too awful to watch. Khalia, however, adjusted the potato sack on her head and sharpened her vision.

Blue flowers?

She couldn't remember noticing such a clump on her property before. That color—where had she seen it?—a sort of silvery blue, as of early-morning mist rising off a pond.

"Shredder, it's the kits! Look, in the field."

Shredder's eyes flew open.

They were there, all three of them, huddled in their usual mound, giving off a more powerful radiance than usual, a shine that deepened, it seemed to Shredder, as the bulldozer rumbled toward them.

The machine's heavy treads crushed the forest floor. Its big shovel plowed up the earth. The kits were beyond rescue. Once more they cowered in the path of death. Once again, Shredder cringed in horror. And then, at the very last second, an amazing thing happened.

A clanking sound came from the bulldozer's motor and its body began to shake. Its pace slowed and changed to a lurching wobble. With an ear-splitting shriek, the machine came to a halt. A man stepped out and kicked one of the treads.

Khalia Koo gave a hiss of astonishment.

"Did you ss-see that? It bus-ss-sted!"

"I saw it."

"Right in front of the kits. They're ss-saved."

"They seem to be." Shredder felt quivery with relief.

"How did that happen? It's a miracle! If I didn't know better, I'd be tempted to think . . ." Khalia glanced upward suspiciously but the sky was as un-revealing as ever.

"Still, it makes you wonder," she murmured to herself, "if Mother Nature herself is watching out for them. But why would that be? They're only common kittens!"

Shredder wasn't listening. He was climbing backward as fast as possible down the oak's trunk. Khalia Koo tried to climb after him. The potato sack snagged and slowed her down. Such a bother, these disguises! There were times when she was tempted to throw them off and show her real face, shocking as it might be.

In the distance, she spied Shredder's old cat figure leaping a stone wall with amazing vigor. On he went, wild with joy, scampering through bushes, galloping past the bulldozer, making headlong for the beautiful blue flowers in the field.

CHAPTER FIVE

News of the kits' return traveled around the little forest with tremendous speed. In a matter of hours, every cat had heard about it. That night, after the road crew had gone, dozens made their way to Khalia Koo's ruined rat farm for a first-hand view.

There, beneath the light of a full moon, they came across the silent hulk of the bulldozer and

saw the red gash of its treads through the woods. The crushed rat cages were terrifying to behold. What a good thing the rats hadn't still been inside. No one would wish such an end on even a rat!

It was the kittens who were the most astounding, though. They looked just as they always had, as tiny and inseparable, as playful and unknowing. Wherever they had been these past weeks, it had left no mark on them. In high spirits, they raced around Shredder, overjoyed at their reunion and wanting to make up for lost time.

On his side, Shredder brimmed over with happiness, his old cat face shining bright as the moon itself in the night shadows under the trees. Every cat there felt lifted by the sight. A mood of celebration filled the air, as if some important victory had been won, which in a way it had. For once again the kits had survived. They'd done the impossible, beaten the odds. A wary excitement spread through the crowd of cats, a sense that rules had been broken and patterns long in force disturbed.

What did it mean? No cat could answer that. A few gazed skyward as Khalia Koo had done, in case some ghostly paw should be there stirring the heavens into new configurations. None was, at least none that a scruffy, beaten-down highway cat could at that moment detect.

Certainly nothing had changed out on Interstate 95, where the evening rush hour was under way as usual. Streams of vehicles sped past churning up an unbreathable mix of sand and dirt. Tractor-trailers roared by like tornados, crushing whatever was in their paths. Motors whined, gears ground, fumes rose.

Behind a roadside clump of weeds, Murray the Claw and Jolly Roger crouched together, wiping the grit from their eyes and watching for food.

"I thought you said the little dopes were bagged," Jolly Roger complained during a lull in the traffic. They'd just come from spying on the happy celebration in the woods.

"They were! You saw it too," Murray hissed in reply.

"So, what are they doing back? It's embarrassing. They must have somehow got away from AnCon."

"Dumb twids like them? They couldn't get out of a mud puddle if they fell in."

"They must've had help again."

"They're frauds," Murray growled. "Anyone

with half a brain could see it. Something fishy's going on, mark my words. I wouldn't trust them."

"They definitely don't act like any real kittens I've ever seen," Jolly Roger agreed. "Did you watch them trying to run?"

"They can't pounce either. Can't mew right. Can't talk, that's for sure. Haw, there's not one thing special about them. They can't do anything!"

"But . . . somehow they stopped that bulldozer in its tracks." A note of awe had entered Jolly Roger's voice.

"That wasn't them!" Murray exploded. "Don't you start thinking like a moron. What's come over this woods? We used to know the score around here and be able to deal with it. Now we're being brainwashed by a bunch of nursery school drop-offs? It's sad, sad, but you know what? It won't matter in the end."

"It won't?"

"No." Murray leaned over and whispered in Jolly Roger's ear. "I know a secret!"

"What?"

"This forest is dead wood."

"You mean . . ."

"That's right—we're scorched earth, headed for asphalt."

"Asphalt! How do you know?"

Murray nodded wisely. "I've seen machines like that one in the field before. They mean one thing: a road is going through."

"But the bulldozer broke down!"

"So? It'll get fixed. That dozer will be up and running by tomorrow, you watch. Nothing in the world can stop a road from going through once it's started. Not mountains or rivers, not prairies or deserts, not a jungle full of wild animals and certainly not a bunch of dopey kiddens."

Jolly Roger wilted a bit after hearing this, as if he might have put some hope in the kits himself.

"How about heading up the road for breakfast?" he said, to change the subject. "The moon's going down. It'll be morning soon. We'll get the first pick of jelly doughnuts."

Murray nodded. "Good idea! My favorite's raspberry. What's yours?"

"Peach yogurt," Jolly Roger replied. "It just went on the menu at Hamburger Heaven. Supposed to thicken your hair."

"Yogurt!" Murray shivered all over. "I'd rather eat glue!"

The two cats slouched off into the shadows.

• • •

If only a full moon casting silvery light on a peaceful meadow in a forgotten woods could shine on forever, protecting it and its inhabitants from change.

If only night would never end and the sun would never rise on a highway racing with cars, over a shopping center opening its doors for another frantic day of business, on a bulldozer waiting for repair so that work could continue on an important access road.

This was the wish—the prayer, really—that Shredder found running through his head as he lay beside the sleeping kits in the lost graveyard on the hill.

He and Khalia had brought the kits there to rest after the evening's celebration. Now, as the moon sank down one side of the wood and rosy paws of sun began to creep up the other, Shredder watched over them, making sure no falling leaf or wandering beetle would disturb them. Miraculous they might be, but they were also tiny kittens, fragile and unaware. Shredder wanted more than anything to keep them safe.

Nearby, curled up in various bushes and hollows between the gravestones, other highway cats slept, their dirty tails and broken whiskers giving evidence of their hard lives.

Why were they here? Because they couldn't keep away. Like hungry birds drawn to a spring-time feeder, they were staying close to the kits. The little ones' strange sparkly sheen was now visible to all. Through the dark it glowed, an eerie, other-worldly beacon that seemed to those watching no more or less than the glimmer of hope.

Shredder sighed. The truth was, the future looked grim. An impossible series of miracles would be necessary to save their bit of forest. The old cat knew the signs of road-building as well as Murray the Claw. He knew the power of its ma-chinery and the force of will behind it. Somewhere in the city, high up in one of the office buildings Shredder had passed on his recent journey, a plot had been hatched. A script had been written that could not be unwritten. The stage had been set. Their wood would soon become another strip of roadside brush.

"What's-ss wrong?" Khalia Koo's hiss came sud-denly from overhead. She was perched on the crum-bling stone wall that ran around the graveyard.

"Nothing."

"You shivered. I thought you might have heard something."

"I was remembering another time, another place." Shredder's voice trailed away. "There was a small house, a yard, miles of open land . . ."

"Your old home."

"Yes. I still dream of it sometimes. I had a family once, you know, a bunch of little ones like these." He curled his weathered tail more closely around the sleeping kits. "They've brought it all back, much as I've tried to forget."

"I guess-ssed there was something like that in your past," Khalia said. "I never did see you as a hard-bitten road cat."

"Oh, I've been hard-bitten, all right. I've got the scars to prove it. But I never was as tough as I pretended to be. I've been scared most of the time. I didn't want this highway life. I got lost is what happened, and I couldn't go back."

Khalia became silent, for this was exactly what had happened to her. Shredder's honesty pierced the wall she kept around her heart. Again she felt a desire to throw off her disguise and tell her true story. *"I was once a loved cat who had great beauty and many admirers,"* she would begin. But then what? How would she dare to show her real face? Her burns were so terrible. Shredder would shut his eyes and run.

A metallic shriek sounded from the clearing below, followed by the cough of an engine.

"They're going to fix it," Khalia said. "They're working on it now."

"Only a matter of time," Shredder agreed.

"I guess it's back to the highway for us. We're being ss-shoved out again."

The truth of this remark caught Shredder like a punch in the stomach: the unfairness of it, the careless crushing of small lives, the cringing along roadsides and hiding in weeds, choking on fumes and fighting for road food. It was too much to bear. No one, not even a highway cat, should have to live that way.

"No! I won't do it," he muttered.

"Won't do what?"

"I won't go back out there. I'm too old."

Khalia stared down at him.

"And the kits are too young," Shredder went on wearily. "Miracles or not, they're unfit for the road. We're staying put. This will be our last stop."

"But you can't stay here!" Khalia Koo jumped off the stone wall. "They're going to level this wood. If you think the kits will stop them, good luck is all I can say. This has gone far beyond what anyone can do."

Shredder nodded his old head. "I know, but I'm tired. It's too late to start over. You go on and save yourself. I'll stay with the kits and take what comes. They're the only things I really care about now."

Another wheeze rose from the forest below, followed by the piercing squeal of a motor revving up. Around them, the sleeping highway cats leapt to their feet.

In other parts of the wood, hundreds of birds and wild animals still dozing in the early morning sun also jerked awake. What was that? A storm was coming! All over the wood, warning calls went out and the age-old rustle of frantic preparations could be heard. Bad weather on the way! Get ready! Get ready!

Meanwhile, the three kittens slept on in the Potter graveyard, seemingly unaware of what was happening around them. Mounded together, their heads nestled on each others' backs and their paws curled beneath, they looked to Shredder like a silvery patch of forest floor, the kind of enchanted place a woodland makes when left alone, undisturbed. As the sound of falling trees and tearing turf came to his ears from below, the old cat stayed beside the kittens, drawing warmth from their small bodies and waiting for what was to come.

CHAPTER SIX

To those traveling by car on Interstate 95 that early spring morning,
a strange sight now presented itself.
From the woods along the highway,
clusters of animals began to appear.

A mother skunk and her babies scuttled up
the shoulder of the road. Two raccoons lumbered
out of the brush, blinked at the passing traffic and
scooted away toward the overpass.

Squirrels darted here and there, unable to hold
a straight course but keeping generally to one side
of the traffic. Not so a fox, who zipped like a red-
tailed arrow between the cars, somehow managing

to cross all four lanes of eastbound traffic before landing safely on the center median.

He was followed by five deer and a fawn leaping gracefully lane to lane, crossing the center strip without pause to take on the westbound lanes. Tires screeched. Startled motorists slowed and gaped through their windows. On the heels of the deer came the streaking fox again, dodging bravely between the cars, his slender jaw clenched in fright.

All that morning, animals came out of the little wood to hop, waddle, scamper, pad, skitter, leap and hustle along the eastbound lanes or to make desperate rushes across the highway. Overhead, birds also were evacuating. Hawks and owls, woodpeckers and starlings, robins and early-arriving swallows, even a family of migrating Canada geese flapped away to other sanctuaries, if any were to be had in that congested landscape.

The only animals not seen along the road, for once, were highway cats. And this was because, despite all of Khalia's warnings, most had refused to budge from the old cemetery. They were hunkered down amid the gravestones, sniffing the bulldozer's gritty fumes, listening to its mash and roar through the trees.

In the end, Khalia found that she couldn't leave either. If Shredder was staying, so would she! A strange stubbornness on this point had risen up inside her, though she was the last to see it for what it was. As the morning wore on, she remained, dozing, on the stone wall. Below her, Shredder had fallen into a sound snooze, exhausted from his night of watching over the kits, who continued their nap beside him.

Both cats awoke suddenly about mid-afternoon. All sound of machinery below had stopped. Silence broke like a long, peaceful sigh over the woods. In the distance, a hunting hawk's triumphant shriek pierced the air. From a closer place came the rustle of a small animal scurrying through weeds. Then, just as Shredder's ears had grown accustomed to the quiet, new vibrations rose from the ground. Footsteps. They moved steadily up the hill toward the graveyard. Someone was coming!

Perhaps the kits heard it too. They chose this moment to at last wake up, to sniff, stretch, and look sleepily around.

"Not now!" Shredder whispered to them. "Stay out of sight!"

He pushed their fuzzy heads down.

They didn't understand and pushed back. More dangerously, they decided to become playful. They began to wrestle with each other and to leap.

"Stop that!" Shredder hissed. "For your own good, lie down and be quiet."

It was no use. The kits were now wide awake, and like all young things cooped up for too long, they were surging with energy. The closer the footsteps came, the rowdier they became. They twisted, heaved and squirmed to get away. There was only one thing to do: like a mother hen on her nest, Shredder sat on them. And just in time!

Three orange hard hats appeared not forty feet away, stamping through the grove of tall pine trees near the barn foundation. The cats hidden in the graveyard lowered their heads until only the glimmer of their eyes showed above the weeds. Not a tail twitched. Not a whisker flicked.

The hard-hats paused and glanced around in surprise. An old foundation? A field of crumbling gravestones? One worker brought out a square of paper and consulted it with a frown.

What a nuisance—no mention here of obstacles, his expression announced. And also: *No time for this!*

He waved the others forward. The men went to work pounding red pegs in a wide path across the middle of the cemetery. A roar came from the bull-dozer below as it began to grind uphill. The access road was going through!

At this moment, a violent struggle erupted under Shredder. The kits churned furiously, mewed and squeaked, pushed and pried, and finally broke free by lifting the old cat's body completely off the ground. Who would have guessed they had such strength? They bolted from underneath him into the sun and rolled in a silly tumble through the gravestones to the very feet of the hard-hats, who leaned over for a closer look.

Shredder let out a howl, but it was too late. Hands were already reaching out, scooping up the tiny kittens, holding them high in the air. Beside him, Khalia Koo's eyes flashed sapphire through the potato sack mesh. In a second, she had jumped off the wall and was racing tooth and claw to the rescue. As she ran, the potato sack flapped and crackled around her and began to drag along the ground. Khalia pulled at it desperately, but the sack snagged on the branches of a small bush. For a moment, she was trapped and struggled to break free.

Then, with a frantic hiss, she threw the sack off her head. When she leapt forward again, the cats watching in the graveyard caught their breaths. Under the sun's blazing spotlight, the ruined landscape of her face was plainly revealed. Ragged ridges and deep cracks, bald patches and fibrous scars were all that remained of her once-great beauty.

To her credit, Khalia never broke stride. On she went, strong and unflinching, and this produced an unforeseen result. The hard-hats took one look at the hideous creature bounding toward them and dropped the kits. They staggered back and turned to run. At this, Shredder jumped out with a frightful snarl. In a flash, the other highway cats rose from their hiding places to follow him. A savage swarm of fur-coated monsters catapulted out of the graveyard on the heels of the hard-hats, who yelled in terror and fled down the hill toward the parking lot. Even this wasn't far enough. On the men ran between the cars, to the Three-Minute Egg Roll, where they flung open the door and rushed inside.

What a charge! What a chase! What an amazing turnabout! Never had any cat there felt such a rush of excitement. It was as if they'd been living undercover for years and were suddenly set free to show their real selves. No one wanted to stop! They might have hurtled on into the jaws of death if Khalia's fierce command hadn't brought them to a halt at the edge of the parking lot. Just in time, the cats came to their senses and veered back into the forest. They made for the shelter of the cemetery in a joyful surge.

There was not one second to trade war stories. They were barely inside the old stone wall when footsteps could be heard coming up the hill again.

"Take cover!" Khalia warned. A minute later, a much larger group of hard-hats entered the graveyard and began to look around for what had frightened the first bunch. Once again, the cats hid in the weeds. So well did they make themselves invisible (this time even the kits were quiet as mice) that not a whisker or a tail was seen between the gravestones, and the men went away looking mystified and uneasy.

That afternoon, to the delight of the cats, the bulldozer at the bottom of the hill didn't start up again.

Potterberg Evening News

HAUNTED CEMETERY HALTS ROAD CREW; OFFICIALS INVESTIGATE

A crew of town road builders was reportedly set upon and terrorized this afternoon by unknown attackers in a long-forgotten cemetery along Interstate 95.

The crew was clearing land for a new access road to serve the Potterberg Shopping Center, west of town, when the assault began. Some workers interviewed said whirling devils descended without warning and appeared to rise out of the graves themselves.

"It was terrifying!" one worker reported. "We all ran for our lives. I believe the place is haunted!"

Mayor J. M. Blunt, appearing before reporters with his chief of staff

Milton Farley, urged the community to remain calm.

"We are in the process of investigating this incident, which I'm sure has a logical explanation," he said. "I encourage residents to go ahead with their shopping at the Potterberg Shopping Center.

The area is being monitored for security. Police see no immediate danger to life, limb or the pursuit of business as usual. Shoppers are urged to contact authorities should they encounter any further disturbance."

CHAPTER SEVEN

The victory of the cats over the highway construction crew was so unexpected that at first no cat could believe it.

Even after the second road crew had gone away, wary silence continued in the graveyard and all eyes remained watchful. At last, a few cats crept from their hiding places to sniff the air. Others slunk forward to peer down the hill. "All clear!" they signaled with a wave of tails. Then the rest

straggled out to see for themselves and begin the task of smoothing their rumpled coats.

The kits! Where are the kits? A cry went up. Everyone looked for those tiny balls of fur, those helpless babies whose strange appearance among them had so far brought such a change of fortune.

A short distance away, the little ones were spotted with Shredder. They were in high spirits, scampering under the trees, leaping off the stone walls, clawing each other playfully and acting, as usual, like the most ordinary of kittens.

No one looking at them would think they were at all special. No one would guess they could change anything, much less inspire a mass of down-and-out cats to drive off an official road-building crew. For this, all believed, was what the kits had done. As dusk fell, the cats crept near the little ones and set up watch again. When Shredder mentioned that the kittens might be hungry, a dozen cats sped away to the Dumpsters to forage.

Later, while the kits dined royally on shrimp rolls, other cats made them a mossy bed between some gravestones. Only after all three were tucked in and had fallen asleep did the highway cats close their own eyes and take some much needed rest for themselves.

In this way, several days passed. No sound came from the clearing below. The road workers didn't return, though at every hour they were expected and dreaded. The bulldozer remained where it was, looming silently over the chewed-up path of forest floor. The cats steered clear of it. Most hardly dared venture from the graveyard at all. Only hunger could bring them down the hill to the Dumpsters. (The highway seemed too far to go.) A quick bite and they padded back to set up watch again, drawn by the kits' mysterious sparkle.

It was in the evening that this enchanting phenomenon was most visible. The velvety darkness of the little forest drew close around their glowing mound, magnifying it to a jewel-like brilliance. By this light, pine needles seemed to give off a new and intoxicating fragrance, the wind became musical, the air turned silvery with spring dew and a delicious peace descended. If this wasn't magic, nothing was, and every cat there knew it. They had not properly appreciated the little wood before, they saw.

They did now.

Though most among them had never known the comfort of a family, they felt something like it as they bedded down together around the kittens in the graveyard and dropped off to sleep one by one.

Curled on his side near the kits, gazing at a far-off sparkle of stars, Shredder also was swept by a deep contentment. For the first time in many years, he felt a sense of belonging that came close to how he'd felt in his lost home. The evening air seemed as soft here as it had been there. The sky was as wide and mysterious. Spring was coming, as it always would, dependable as the sun that rose every morning. How he loved this old earth for its ancient and beautiful ways.

These happy thoughts were followed by such a pang of sadness, however, that the old cat laid his head abruptly on his paws.

"What's wrong?"

Khalia Koo sat nearby, ever alert to his moods.

"Nothing."

"I thought you might feel ill." She came over to him. Through the murk of night, her profile was barely visible, and that was just as well. She had given up wearing her containers. What was the use of hiding her face when the others had seen it anyway? She was ugly. So be it. Somehow she must learn to live with her disgrace.

"I was just realizing," Shredder replied, "how

all this will be gone soon: the trees, the smells, the wind, the darkness. I'm glad I won't be around to miss them."

"Won't be around?"

"Time is passing. I've grown old."

"Don't be silly," Khalia snapped. "You mustn't talk that way. There's too much to do and . . . you're more important than you think. To the kits, for instance, and all the cats here. And also . . ." She paused. "You're important to me."

"To you?" Shredder's head jerked up in surprise.

"Yes." She held her breath after this admission.

Shredder peered at her doubtfully through the gloom. It was the last thing he could have expected. Now, looking at her, he realized something he must have known all along, even before she'd thrown away her containers.

"Khalia," he told her, "I hope you won't mind if I say that I think you're still very beautiful."

Against all her business principles, Khalia's eyes welled up. Here were the words she'd been longing for. "Shredder . . ." she whispered, and couldn't go on.

It didn't matter. They both understood. There was no need for either to pretend anymore. They'd seen through each other's masks and poses. They were two of a kind, whatever happened next. And whatever happened next, they'd be in it together.

For some time after this, they sat silent atop the cemetery wall while overhead the stars seemed to sparkle with applause.

"I ss-saw the road builders today," Khalia said, drawing herself up finally. "They were in the parking lot behind the shopping center unloading new machines. I think they'll be here tomorrow."

"Well, we bought ourselves a little time," Shredder said. "It was nice while it lasted."

"Yes," Khalia agreed, "and I've been thinking about that. How would it be if we bought ourselves a little more?"

"A fine idea, but not likely," Shredder said.

Khalia's tail twitched. "You mentioned, I think, that Murray the Claw owed you a favor? Well, I've requested one on your behalf."

"What could Murray possibly do for us? He's down on the highway with Jolly Roger, gorging himself on road food."

"Exactly. In perfect position!"

She'd spoken too loudly. Below her, the sleeping kits were disturbed. They lifted their tiny heads and looked directly at her, then they glanced around for Shredder. Discovering him right beside them, they reassembled in their luminous mound and fell back asleep.

"What have you asked Murray to do?" Shredder whispered.

"To bring us disguises!" Khalia's intelligent eyes glowed with pleasure. "Containers of all kinds, soup to nuts, cereal to cottage cheese. They're down there on the highway, you know, by the hundreds."

"But how . . . ?"

"Scare tactics, Shredder. It worked once, why not again?"

She had no more time to explain because at that moment a bustle of movement interrupted their conversation. The overburdened shapes of two large cats appeared. They entered the graveyard through a break in the stone wall, dragging a mass of stuff behind them.

"Murray the Claw, is that you?" Khalia hissed through the dark.

"Yes, id's me, who else?" came his nasty, nasal growl. "Where do you want us to dump this garbage?"

●●●●●●●●●●●●●●●

SCENE: Potterberg city hall, high up in Mayor Blunt's office. His Honor stands at the window gazing at a distant cluster of roofs: the shopping center. He frowns and waves a hand in the air as he speaks to Chief of Staff Farley.

MAYOR BLUNT. So what's the problem? There's nothing up in that graveyard, is there?

FARLEY. No, sir. Not that anyone can see. We've had a surveillance team watching it the past few days. All they've observed is a few stray cats coming and going.

MAYOR. Well, let's get a move on with this road project! Time is running out. The election is in a couple of weeks!

FARLEY. Yes, sir. I've ordered the road crew to start up again. They should be going in this morning. They're a little nervous, some of them, after that business with the ghosts or whatever.

MAYOR. Ghosts! Bah! What nonsense.

FARLEY. Right. Absolutely. But (*worriedly*) there have been suggestions put forward that maybe we should be thinking twice about—

MAYOR. (*Cutting Farley off*) Building a road

through a graveyard? Hogwash! I didn't hear any protests when we laid out our plans. Nobody's cared about that patch of brambles out there for fifty years! It's the scaredy-cat road crew. Fire them! Get somebody in there that can do the job.

FARLEY. Yes, sir! I mean, no, sir, this crew will do it. They're starting this morning, like I said. The road is going through. We won't have any more trouble.

MAYOR. Good work, Farley. You're my man. Now on to more important matters. Have my campaign signs been put up yet? "Blunt Is Better!" "Blunt Is Blunter!" "Blunt Gets the Point!" Which slogan carries my message best?

FARLEY. (*Looking tired.*) All of them—you're a winner for sure.

CHAPTER EIGHT

The sun had barely risen the next day when the startup roar of an engine ripped like an explosion into the peaceful hush of the little forest. It was joined by a second roar and a third until the air itself seemed to scream in pain.

The noise came from the shopping center parking lot. A small army of men had gathered there during the predawn hours and was now ready, with a battery of earthmoving machines, to advance on the woods. The men's boots were laced, their hard hats were strapped down and their faces were

grim, as if they really were soldiers about to enter a combat zone.

Khalia Koo, watching from the top of one of the tall pine trees that grew near the cemetery, smiled her knowing Siamese smile. The hard-hats were scared of the forest. This boded well for her plan. She signaled with her tail to Shredder below: *They're coming!*

"As if that weren't obvious!" growled Murray the Claw to Jolly Roger. The two cats were huddled together behind the cemetery's stone wall, keeping a cynical eye on the proceedings.

"It's sad, sad how Khalia and Shredder have got everyone believing they can beat the odds," Murray went on. "Rejects conquer the world! Highway trash fights back! Who would you put your bet on?"

Jolly Roger grinned his gruesome grin.

Around them, an extraordinary scene was taking place. Several dozen highway cats were attempting to rig themselves out in what appeared to be, in fact, rubbish. Tissue boxes and cracker boxes, chip bags and burger wrappers, fried chicken tubs and paper cups, takeout food containers and instant cocoa packets were just a few of the items that were being snatched up by the cats and tried on for size. They came from the pile of trash that Murray and Roger had brought up from the highway the night before.

More than a few cats had already chosen their getups. They were hard at work gnawing eyeholes, a tricky task requiring concentration (and a lot of spitting so as not to swallow) to get the spacing right. Khalia, an expert at this, had shown them the technique. She herself wasn't preparing a disguise.

"I am frightful enough already," she pointed out. No cat disputed her. She was outstandingly horrible to look at even at that moment as she climbed down the pine tree to stand among them. One or two cats backed away, still shocked by her appearance, but a larger number crowded around to hear what she had to say.

"Our plan of attack is as follows," she began. "We'll lie low until the road crew is just outside the graveyard. When I give the first signal, it would be best if everyone could howl. Can you do that?"

A few of the younger cats, delighted by this invitation, began to yawp and meowl in excruciating tones at the top of their lungs. The effect was ghastly. The older cats flattened their ears.

"Excellent! That's just what we want," Khalia told them. "Much more of the same from you all, please."

She went on: "At my second signal, there must be another round of howls with the addition of some wailing screams. Imagine that you are sinking slowly into quicksand or, better yet, being ambushed by coyotes."

The cats shivered and glanced over their shoulders at the mention of coyotes. They had lost friends to those awful beasts and didn't like even to hear them mentioned.

"Watch closely because after this, I will give a third signal," Khalia said. "It will be the call to rise. We must stand up and move together in our disguises, no one rushing ahead. This is very important. Together, we will terrify the road workers. Singly, we'll have no effect whatever. Is this understood?"

It was. By now, most cats had put on their containers and were hardly recognizable as cats at all except for those telltale lengths of fur protruding from beneath.

"All tails out of sight," Khalia warned, gazing with satisfaction at the stinking heap of four-legged trash standing in front of her. "We are no longer what we were. We are now what we have never been: an apparition of horror!"

Jolly Roger was leaning forward in fascination listening to this.

"What's an apparition?" he whispered to Murray the Claw. "I think I'd like to be one!"

"Don't be stupid, Stupid! It's just a fancy name for a ghost. This is all a buildup to catastrophe," Murray hissed. "Come away with me or you're sure to get caught."

On the other side of the graveyard, Shredder was saying the same thing to the kits. The little scamps were in one of their playful moods. They had found an old egg carton and were parading around underneath it caterpillar style. Only their twelve tiny feet showed out the bottom, a sight hardly calculated to terrify anyone.

"Stop that right now," Shredder warned them. "We must go before it's too late. This is no place for kittens. You'll only get trampled."

It was no use. They wouldn't follow directions. Soon it really was too late. Heavy footsteps and a thundering tread of machinery could be heard coming uphill. Shredder collared the egg carton and yanked it behind a gravestone. The other cats lowered themselves, and their disguises, into the high grass.

Closer the noise came, closer and closer. All eyes were trained on Khalia's Siamese tail, an elegant, dark ribbon rising up through the long grass. A gritty smell of hot machinery swirled like a dust storm into the graveyard. The kits sneezed. The cats coughed. Would the signal never come?

It came.

Above the weeds, Khalia Koo's tail waved like a gallant flag.

A bloodcurdling howl poured from the throat of every cat in the graveyard, a sound so heartfelt and penetrating that it cut through the roar of a bulldozer just then cresting the hill.

A line of approaching hard hats glanced uneasily around. One worker held up his hand to stop the bulldozer. It halted, growling and panting like a leashed dog.

Once again, Khalia's tail flashed in the weeds. The cats let loose with a second howl, a wild crescendo of ghoulish wails and cataclysmic shrieks as if all life on earth were about to come to an end.

The work crew froze at the entrance to the

cemetery. With wide eyes, the men scanned the tangled weeds and vines around the gravestones. When nothing could be seen there, they looked at each other and then, fearfully, up into the sky. Here was the perfect moment for the third signal.

Khalia waved her tail: RISE!

Between the long grasses, the disguised cats came to their feet and began, with slow and steady steps, to move forward across the cemetery. The effect was horrifying, as if a monstrous field of trash had come to life between the graves, a living, breathing tide of furious-eyed garbage that slobbered and hissed and slithered toward the road crew.

"HELP!"

"RUN!"

The workers didn't wait to ask what kind of apparition this could possibly be. They fled, pushing and yelling and tripping over each other. Caught in the retreat, two bulldozers, a dump truck and a front loader reversed gear and accelerated at top speed down the hill. The machines roared backward through the little woods and, following close behind the running workers, heaved back onto the parking lot, where they flattened several parked cars in their haste to get across. The mangling sounds of these collisions rebounded back to the cemetery with a satisfying echo. Several cats peered out from under their disguises.

"Are they gone?"

"They are!"

"Did we do it?"

"We did!"

"Hooray! Hooray!" The monster wave of trash wobbled and toppled and began to break apart. For a moment, rubbish flew in all directions. Then the transformation was complete: tubs and cups, bags and wrappers became again the heads and tails of ecstatic cats. They surrounded Khalia Koo and Shredder in a wild surge and, before they could protest, pulled the kits from their egg carton and lifted them high off the ground.

"Put them down! You'll crush them!" Shredder cried in alarm.

"If you want to thank someone, thank me!" Khalia sniffed.

The cats did thank her. They loved and extolled her. They loved Shredder too. And they loved each other. Hadn't they all worked together to pull the thing off? Together! Think of it. Without a scratch or hiss. This in itself was a kind of miracle. Something wonderful was in motion, some fantastic, cosmic change, and everyone, even Khalia, agreed on who was responsible.

"IT'S THOSE KIDDENS AGAIN!" Murray the Claw growled to Jolly Roger. The two were watching the victory parade from one of the fallen timbers of the old barn. "Look at them riding around like royalty in a coach. If you want my opinion, everybody in this forest is being taken to the cleaners. They've fallen in headfirst and are going down the drain. Their noses are getting skinned, their fur is being fleeced, they've swallowed hook, line and sinker and now they're headed for the soup."

No one knew more ways to describe life's tricks and treacheries than Murray the Claw, probably because he'd suffered more than most in his time. He looked around for Jolly Roger after making this dark prediction, but Roger was nowhere to be seen. A moment later, as Murray scowled down on the celebration below, he caught sight of the yellow cat sidling up to the kits with a greasy grin.

"Why, you double-crossing road rat!" Murray exclaimed. "You've gone and joined up with those nidwid phonies."

Potterberg Evening News

CEMETERY PHANTOMS STRIKE AGAIN!

For the second time in a week, a team of road builders has been set upon and terrorized by ghostly attackers. The assault occurred as workers once again approached an old cemetery that lies in the path of an access road being constructed to the Potterberg Shopping Center. Several victims reported that a massive field of what appeared to be roadside litter rose up to confront them as they came toward the graveyard.

"We couldn't believe it," said Jim King, project foreman. "There was howling first, then a bunch of eerie screams. Then we saw a tidal wave of trash coming at us, steaming and stinking to high heaven. And the scary thing was it had eyes, hundreds of eyes! We got out of there fast."

"If you ask me, it was spirits of the dead sending us a message," added Larry Turpin, who twisted an ankle during the retreat. "We shouldn't be building a road through there. That's old Potter land, and it's their graves we're bothering."

Town officials, including Mayor Blunt, played down the comments.

"What we've got here is a childish case of overactive imagination," Blunt told reporters. "There are no ghosts in that place. My guess is the wind blew some trash up from the highway and scared a few folks. My intention is to replace that road crew with one that can finish the job. The road is going through!"

Opposition to the access road is gaining strength, however, and with the election only a week a way, some residents seem ready to vote against the mayor if he doesn't take the matter more seriously.

CHAPTER NINE

That night, a spring rainstorm blew through the forest. In the cemetery at the top of the hill, the cats took cover. The wind whipped between the gravestones like a ghostly broom, sweeping up the litter of trash left lying there. Down the hill the rubbish flew, back to the highway, where the wheels of passing vehicles soon mashed it to a papery pulp. No evidence remained of Kahlia Koo's ingenious trash disguises.

When the cats woke in the morning, they found

the cemetery tidied up corner to corner and sparkling in the sun. The air had a dazzling freshness to it. The chirp of songbirds came from the trees overhead. During the night, several flocks had flown in to shelter in the lower branches. And this was just the first flutter of woodland life that now began to return to the forest.

Soon animals of all kinds could be seen slipping back to their old territories. A busload of commuters on the highway witnessed the homecoming of the red fox, joined now by a mate, as both scampered across the traffic lanes. A little later, seven deer made the sprint in safety. A pair of raccoons rose from a culvert near the overpass and waddled with low-slung determination down the shoulder of the road.

Something was calling from the little wood. Some ancient force of nature was drawing them back, though its lines of power were invisible and mysterious. A telepathic signal was being sent and received. *They are gone! You are safe! Come home. Come home.*

Uphill in the graveyard, the highway cats heard it too. They sat alert along the stone walls watching and listening as the forest filled once more with familiar sounds. Out on the highway, the roar of traffic was as loud as ever, but to the cats it seemed distant. Here, inside the wood, more important projects were under way. The business of living was taking charge again. Nests were being built. Berries were being stockpiled. Babies were being born. The wild cry of the hawk echoed in triumph through the air.

Though only a few days had passed since the road crew's bulldozer had cut its first path across the forest floor, already tiny grass shoots and vines were plotting to reclaim their old places. Trees and bushes were thickening with leaves. Flowers thrust up through the trampled ground and bloomed. Nature was on the rise, taking back what was hers. "Come home," earth was calling. "We'll win in the end."

ON THE STONE WALL, listening with the other highway cats, Khalia Koo's Siamese eyes shone bright in her ravaged face.

"Something's happening," she told Shredder in a low voice. "I can't tell exactly what, but there's been a change."

"I feel it too," he answered. "A new smell is in the air. Do you think it's possible . . . ?" He stopped, afraid of putting his hope into words.

Khalia wasn't so careful. "Why not?" she asked. "We've come this far. I've been thinking I'd like to start a new business. I had a vision just now of going into catnip: catnip tea, catnip cake, catnip air scent and soap. Catnip," she went on "is quite easily grown, far more manageable than rats in terms of packaging and transport."

Shredder twitched his tail. "I'm not sure canned rat would have sold anyway. Fresh ones are so available on every street corner these days."

"What would you do with a little more time here?" Khalia asked him.

Shredder shook his old head. He glanced down at the kits, still happily asleep in their mound. "I suppose I might go into rescue work," he answered finally.

"Rescuing what?"

"Well, anything, everything, from the highway out there. The fact is, any one of these highway drop-offs might grow up to be something special."

"A sure way to get killed," Khalia grumbled, but she glanced at him in admiration.

These were not the only hopes circulating

in the graveyard that morning. All the cats were heartened by the hustle and bustle of returning life around them. Perhaps they weren't ready to believe it would last, however, for they continued to keep watch over the kits, as if they held the magic key to it all. This was why, when the little ones finally awoke from their night's sleep on that sparkling morning after the storm, the highway cats were alarmed to see them acting so strangely.

SHREDDER NOTICED IT FIRST. "I don't know what's wrong. They're limp," he said.

"They're just tired," snapped Khalia, who had more pressing matters on her mind. "We're all tired. Yesterday was a tremendous victory. Look, there's no sign of the road crew this morning! We must not make the mistake of resting on our laurels. It's all very well to sit around and hope, but there's nothing like action for clinching the deal."

Shredder was too worried to think of action or deals.

"They have no bounce, no jump, no spirit," he went on. "It's totally unlike them. And their color is bad. They've turned mouse gray."

"I'm sure they'll be better after a good solid

meal," Khalia said. "I'll send out for meatballs and shrimp from the Dumpsters."

She dispatched a group of cats who were hanging around staring at the little ones' odd behavior. They were back with the food inside of an hour, but here was another surprise. The kits refused to eat.

"This has never happened before," Shredder said darkly. "They've eaten like horses ever since they arrived. What can be wrong?"

Khalia Koo was impatient. She had no time to waste on the sniffles of babies. A second attack from the parking lot might come at any moment. Who knew what the road crew would think of next? They might decide to invade from the highway or drop in by helicopter. Such things had happened in other forests, she had heard.

"These kits need fresh air and exercise," she counseled Shredder. "Get them up and out. They'll be back to normal soon."

Shredder tried. The kittens paid no attention. They didn't want to climb. They didn't want to play. They drifted around like tiny zombies. Worst of all, they kept wandering toward the highway, as if they'd forgotten its treacherous ways. Twice Shredder had to run after them and bring them back.

By afternoon, the old cat was exhausted, and Khalia wasn't around to help. She was setting up nocturnal patrols in the woods bordering the parking lot in case an attack should come by night.

"Can we be of some assistance?" one of the larger alley cats asked Shredder. "We'd be honored to watch the kits while you have a nap."

Shredder sighed and nodded. "Don't let them go near the highway," he warned. Then he went behind the stone wall and fell asleep.

By the time Khalia returned, night had fallen. It was she who discovered that the kits were gone. Their sleeping nest was cold. They hadn't been in it for some time.

"We put them to bed!" exclaimed the guilty cat sitters. "They were sound asleep when we last checked! It's not our fault! They must have snuck off when we weren't looking!"

Khalia put out a call for help. There was no reason to think they had gone very far. "We'll find them," she assured the frantic highway cats. She contacted a flock of crows to help with aerial scouting.

An hour later, the kittens had still not been seen.

Shredder awoke from his nap to widespread

panic. Everyone was in the woods, beating bushes and climbing trees.

"Come here, little miracles," the highway cats mewed. "Stop teasing us. Come back and play."

At this moment, Shredder had a terrible thought.

"Has anyone checked the highway?" he asked Khalia.

"The highway! They surely won't be there!"

"They were trying to go all morning," he informed her. "Something was very wrong with them. In all the weeks they've been here, they've never acted like this."

"Go there, quickly." Khalia pushed him along. "If they'll come to anyone, it will be you, my love."

RAIN HAD BEGUN TO fall again when Shredder arrived at the highway. The pavement was slick and greasy-looking. Though the night was dark, a bloodred glow lit the underside of the storm clouds overhead. It came from the blazing city of Potterberg in the distance.

Shredder crouched along the roadside. Many days had passed since he'd last been here, and the roar of traffic hurt his ears. A double tractor-trailer blasted past his nose. A mail truck went by, then a lopsided furniture van. Chilly winds began to blow. He was about to move farther up the road toward the overpass when a rustle sounded from the weeds nearby. The vicious profile of a large, bristle-hair alley cat rose from a bush.

"So, id's Shredder. Haven't seen you out here for a while."

"Hello, Murray."

"Hello yourself. Whad's going down?"

"Not much. Seen anything out here tonight?"

"Nope. No food to speak of. It's the rain that does it. People don't like to open their windows to throw the stuff out."

"I know."

The two sat gazing across the asphalt.

"There was one thing," Murray growled after a minute. "Now that I think about it, I suppose that's why you're here."

"Why?" Shredder asked.

"For the twids," Murray said. "They came by a while back. I told 'em to go home."

"Did they go?"

"Nope. They wouldn't. I tried to head 'em off. Wasn't nobody looking after them."

"Where'd they go after that?"

For the first time, Murray looked uncomfortable. He glanced up the highway and twitched his ratty tail.

"They went across," he muttered.

"What?"

"Across. Over there."

Shredder's mouth dried up. "Did they make it?"

"Yup. They're out there on the median. I told 'em not to do it. They didn't pay no attention."

And now, as Shredder peered through the rain across the eastbound lanes to the center strip, his heart gave a sickening leap. A tiny shadow came out from a clump of grass. A second later, two other shadows followed, bumbling along in a way that Shredder recognized and that sent a white flash of terror through every nerve in his body.

"Don't move!" he bellowed. "I'm coming to get you."

He would have leapt blindly onto the highway if Murray hadn't reached out and grabbed him by the neck.

"Are you crazy?" Murray asked. "You can't go over there. You'd never make it at your age. Anyway, they don't want you. They're waiting for something. Look!"

Shredder stopped struggling long enough to notice that the kits had come together in one of their luminous blue mounds. They huddled and brightened, their tiny heads turned to look up the highway. For a long minute, nothing happened and nobody moved and time froze.

And then another miracle occurred, something just as strange as the kits' arrival among them. At least that's how Shredder later chose to describe it to Khalia and the others. This time even Murray was too amazed to protest.

Down the road came a pickup truck. As Shredder and Murray watched, it swerved suddenly out of the line of traffic and bounced onto the overgrown center median. The driver stepped out. He lifted a cardboard box from the pickup's cargo bed and stooped down over the kittens. With a single swipe of an enormous hand, he scooped them into the box and tossed it with practiced aim into the back of the truck. Then he got in himself and peeled out with shrieking tires, leaving the stink of hot rubber behind in the air.

・・・・・・・・・・・・・・・・

SCENE: Two weeks later. Potterberg city hall, high up in the mayor's office. His Honor Mayor Blunt stands at the window gazing down fondly upon the bustling city of Potterberg. He is conducting a private conference with Chief of Staff Farley. The roar of traffic comes from outside as usual.

MAYOR BLUNT. Well, Farley, I did it! I won the election.

FARLEY. Good job, sir. We're all proud of you. Potterberg couldn't ask for a better mayor.

MAYOR. It was close, I have to say. That Potterberg Shopping Center access road almost ruined everything. Who would have guessed a hundred-year-old cemetery would cause such a ruckus?

FARLEY. Nobody! You handled it perfectly, though. Canceling the road construction at the last minute, calling in the Historical Society, setting up a plan to preserve that patch of woods in honor of our first family.

MAYOR. Our first family? Who is that?

FARLEY. The Potters, sir. Wasn't it in honor of them that you . . . ?

MAYOR. Oh yes, so I did. Early settlers, heritage, historic land. Voters seem to appreciate that sort of thing these days. Make a note for future elections, Farley. Shopping centers out, cemeteries in.

FARLEY. Right, sir. I've got it.

MAYOR. What do you think about going even further? We could open up that bit of woods to tourists, put up a monument, a visitors center, a merry-go-round for the kids. We could name it after me!

FARLEY. Well, sir, that's a thought. Not much land left to work with out there, though. You might want to be associated with something larger and more important, like a bridge . . .

MAYOR. A bridge. Hmmm. My name over troubled water . . .

FARLEY. Or a sports complex. They're popular these days. You know that swampy stretch of land out by the reservoir? Nothing lives there now but some wild ducks and a few stray cats. We'll get rid of them in a jiffy.

MAYOR. A sports complex! That's it! Farley, you're worth your weight in gold. Let's go to work on it. I'll get the permits; you get the construction crew. People will be impressed!

FARLEY. They'll know you're a mover and a shaker.

MAYOR. So they will, Farley, so they will!

(Outside, traffic noises rise to a bone-jarring roar. As the mayor continues to stand at the window, an anonymous pickup truck zooms past on the highway below, a small cardboard box bouncing in the cargo bed behind the shadowy head of the driver.)

C URTAIN

DATE			